ISBN 0 86112 942 3
Published by Brimax Books Ltd, Newmarket, England 1993.
Printed in Hong Kong.

Alice
IN
WONDERLAND

Lewis Carroll

Illustrated by

Eric Kincaid

BRIMAX · NEWMARKET · ENGLAND

Introduction

Lewis Carroll was the pen-name of mathematics lecturer Charles Dodgson when writing his nonsense poems and books. He was born on 27th January 1832 and was educated at Richmond School, Yorkshire, Rugby School and Christ Church, Oxford, where he taught mathematics for 26 years until 1881.

His best-known book is *Alice in Wonderland* which he wrote specially for the daughter of the Dean of Christ Church. Her name was Alice Pleasance Liddell. The book was first published in 1865 and has since become one of the most famous and best-loved children's stories ever written.

In Lewis Carroll's story, Alice follows the White Rabbit down the rabbit-hole into a wonderland where creatures have never-ending tea-parties and play the strangest game of croquet ever seen.

This specially adapted version of *Alice in Wonderland* has been beautifully illustrated by Eric Kincaid and is sure to delight all children reading about Alice's adventures for the first time.

Contents

Down the Rabbit-hole

Alice was getting very tired of sitting next to
her sister on the bank, with nothing to do. She had
looked at her sister's book, but it had no pictures
in it. Alice did not see the point of a book without
pictures.

Alice was beginning to wonder whether she should
make a daisy-chain, when suddenly a White Rabbit
with pink eyes ran close by her. There was nothing
strange about that, and Alice was not even very
surprised when she heard the Rabbit say to itself,
"Oh dear! I shall be so late!" But when the Rabbit
took a watch out of its waistcoat-pocket, Alice
jumped to her feet and ran across the field after
it. She was just in time to see it pop down a large
rabbit-hole. Alice followed it never giving a
thought as to how she would get out again.

The rabbit-hole went straight on like a tunnel. Suddenly, Alice found herself falling down what seemed to be a very large hole. Either the hole was very deep or she was falling very slowly, for she had plenty of time to look around her as she fell.

At first she tried to look down but it was too dark to see anything. Then she looked at the sides, and noticed they were filled with cupboards and bookshelves. She took down a jar from one of the shelves as she passed. It was labelled "ORANGE MARMALADE" but it was empty. She put it into one of the cupboards as she fell past.

Down, down, down. Would the fall never come to an end? "I wonder how many miles I have fallen?" said Alice to herself. "I must be near the centre of the earth by now. I wonder if I shall fall right through the earth!"

Down, down, down. There was nothing else to do, so Alice started to talk again. "Dinah will miss me very much tonight." (Dinah was her cat.) "I hope they give her a saucer of milk at dinner-time." Alice started to get very sleepy. She felt that she was dozing off, and had just began to dream that she was walking hand in hand with Dinah, when suddenly, thump! Thump! Thump! Down she came upon a heap of dry sticks and leaves. The fall was over.

Alice was not hurt, she jumped to her feet and looked up to see how far she had actually fallen but it was too dark to see anything. In front of her was another long passage. The White Rabbit was hurrying down it. Quickly Alice followed. She heard the Rabbit say as it turned a corner, "Oh my ears and whiskers, how late it is getting!" Alice was close behind as she turned the corner, but the Rabbit had disappeared. She found herself in a long, low hall. There were doors all round the hall, but they were all locked and when Alice had been all the way down one side and up the other trying every door, she walked sadly down the middle wondering how she was ever going to get out again.

Suddenly she came across a three-legged table, made of glass. The only thing on the table was a tiny golden key.

Alice thought that it might belong to one of the doors, she went along trying them all but it would not open any of them. On the second time round she came across a low curtain that she had not noticed before. Behind it there was a little door about fifteen inches high. She tried the little golden key in the lock and to her delight it fitted.

Alice opened the door and found that it led into a small passage, not much larger than a rat-hole. She knelt down and looked along the passage into the loveliest garden you ever saw. She really wished she could walk around the garden but found that she could not even fit her head through the doorway.

"Oh, I wish I was small enough to be able to walk through the door," thought Alice.

There seemed to be no point in waiting by the little door, so she went back to the table, half hoping she might find another key. This time she found a bottle on it.

"How strange!" said Alice, "this was not here before."

Tied around the neck of the bottle was a label, with the words "DRINK ME" printed in large letters.

It was all very well to say "DRINK ME", but Alice was not going to do that in a hurry. "No," she said. "I will look first to see if it is marked poison or not." However this bottle was not marked poison, so Alice tasted it, and finding that she liked it she soon finished it off.

"What a curious feeling!" said Alice. "I'm getting smaller, I must be shutting up like telescope."

She was now only ten inches high, and her face brightened up at the thought that she was now the right size for going through the door into that lovely garden. But when poor Alice got to the door, she found she had forgotten to pick up the little golden key from the table.

She went back to the table and found she could not reach it, she could see it through the glass and she tried her best to climb up one of the legs of the table, but it was too slippery. Poor Alice was worn out with trying so she gave up and sat down and cried.

*She knelt down and looked along the passage into the loveliest
garden you ever saw.*

"What's the point in crying?" she asked herself.
"It's not going to make me any smaller."

She began to look around her and soon her eye
fell on a little glass box that was lying under the
table. She was sure that it hadn't been there before
but she opened it, and found in it a very small
cake, on which the words "EAT ME" were written
in currants.

"Well," said Alice, "if it makes me grow larger,
I can reach the key, and if it makes me grow smaller,
I can creep under the door, so either way I will get
into the garden!"

She ate a little bit, and said anxiously to
herself, "Which way? Which way?" To her surprise she
remained the same size. Alice was so used to strange
things happening to her that she was more surprised
when nothing happened. She carried on eating and
very soon she finished the cake.

The Pool of Tears

"Curiouser and curiouser!" cried Alice. "Now I am opening out like the largest telescope ever! Goodbye feet!"

Just at this moment her head touched the roof of the hall, in fact she was now rather more than nine feet tall. She picked up the golden key and rushed to the little door. Poor Alice! She was much too big to get through the door. She sat down and began to cry again, shedding gallons of tears.

"You should be ashamed of yourself," said Alice to herself. "A great girl like you crying like this."

But Alice could not stop crying, and she cried until there was a large pool all around her, four inches deep and reaching halfway down the hall.

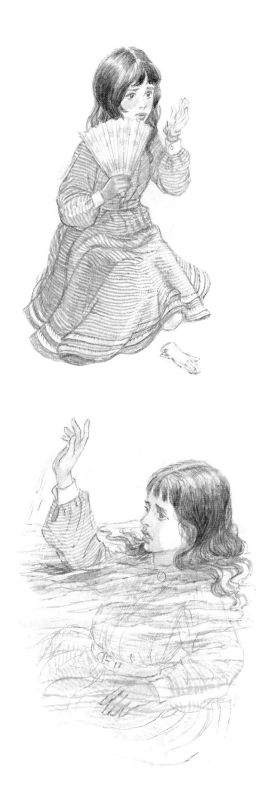

After a time she heard a pattering of feet in the distance, she hastily dried her eyes to see what was coming. It was the White Rabbit returning, dressed very smartly, with a pair of white gloves in one hand and a fan in the other. He came trotting along in a great hurry, muttering to himself as he came, "Oh! The Duchess! Won't she be angry if I've kept her waiting!" Alice felt so desperate that she was ready to ask help of any one, so when the Rabbit came near her, she said in a shy voice, "Excuse me, sir–" The Rabbit jumped with fright, dropped the white gloves and the fan, and ran away into the darkness as fast as he could go.

Alice picked up the fan and the gloves, the hall was very hot so she started to fan herself. She started to talk to herself as she had nothing better to do. "Dear, dear! How strange everything is today! Everything was the same yesterday. Perhaps I have changed in the night."

She looked down at her hands and found that she had put on one of the White Rabbit's gloves.

"How could I have done that?" she thought. "I must be growing small again." She got up and went to the table to measure herself by it and found out that she was only two feet high and shrinking rapidly, she soon found out that the cause of this was the fan and she dropped it quickly, to save herself from shrinking away altogether.

"That was very lucky," thought Alice. "Now for the garden." But when she got there she found the door locked again and the little golden key was on the table. "This is terrible," thought Alice sadly.

As she said this her foot slipped and she found herself up to her neck in salt water. She soon realised that she was in the pool of tears that she had cried when she was nine feet tall.

"I wish I had not cried so much," thought Alice, as she swam about trying to find her way out. Just then she heard some splashing in the pool, she swam nearer to make out what it was. She thought it could be a walrus or a hippopotamus, but then she remembered how small she was and soon found out that a mouse had fallen in the pool as well.

14

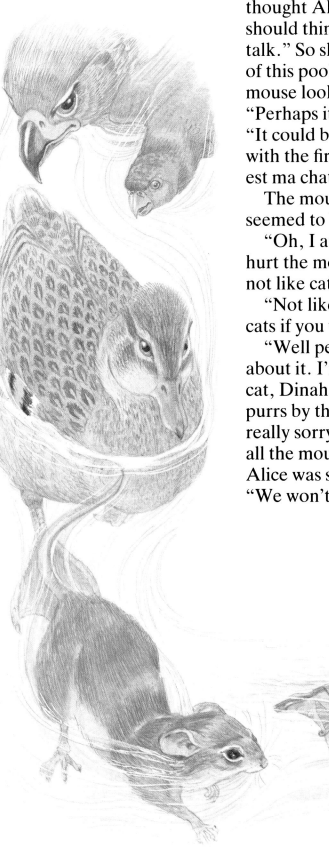

"I wonder if I should speak to this mouse," thought Alice, "everything has been so strange I should think it very likely that it will be able to talk." So she began, "Mouse, do you know the way out of this pool? I am very tired of swimming." The mouse looked at her curiously, but said nothing. "Perhaps it doesn't speak English," thought Alice. "It could be a French mouse." So she began again with the first sentence that came into her head. "Ou est ma chatte?"

The mouse gave a sudden leap out of the water and seemed to be shaking all over with fright.

"Oh, I am sorry," said Alice, afraid that she had hurt the mouse's feelings. "I forgot that mice do not like cats."

"Not like cats!" cried the mouse. "Would you like cats if you were me?"

"Well perhaps not," said Alice. "Do not be angry about it. I'm sure though, that you would like my cat, Dinah. She is a very quiet cat. She sits and purrs by the fire, cleaning her whiskers. Oh, I'm really sorry!" cried Alice again, because this time all the mouse's fur seemed to be standing on end. Alice was sure that she had offended it this time. "We won't talk about her anymore."

15

"We indeed!" cried the mouse, who was trembling down to the end of its tail. "As if I would talk about such a thing! Our family has always hated cats, nasty things. Don't let me hear you mention them again."

"I won't," said Alice, in a great hurry to change the subject. "Are you fond of dogs?"

The mouse did not answer, so Alice continued, "One of our friends is a farmer and he has got the loveliest dog. It kills all the rats – oh, no! I'm very sorry, have I upset you again?"

The mouse had started to swim away from Alice, so she followed it calling, "Mouse! Please come back, I promise not to mention cats or dogs again."

When the mouse heard this, it turned round and slowly swam back to her. It said, "Let us swim to the shore, now."

Alice followed it and was surprised to see that the pool had suddenly become quite crowded with birds and animals that had also fallen in. There was a Duck and a Dodo, a Lory and an Eaglet and several other curious creatures. The whole party swam ashore.

They must have looked a very strange group standing on the shore. The birds' feathers were wet and bedraggled, the animals' fur was wet and clinging to them. They were all dripping wet, cross and uncomfortable.

Everyone started to complain about how wet they were. So the first question was of course, how they should get dry again.

"I think," said the Dodo, "that the best thing to get us dry would be a Caucus-race."

"What is a Caucus-race?" asked Alice.

"Well," said the Dodo. "The best way to describe it is to do it."

First the Dodo marked out a race-course, then all the birds and animals were placed along the course. There was no "Ready – GO!" but they all started to run when they liked, so it was not very easy to tell when the race was over. When they had been running for half an hour or so and were all dry again, the Dodo suddenly called out, "The race is over!"

All the runners crowded round him asking who had won. The Dodo had to think about this answer for a long time. Everyone was silent as the Dodo finally said that they had all won and that they must all have a prize.

"But who is to give the prizes?" asked everyone.

"Why, she of course," said the Dodo pointing to Alice. The whole party crowded round her calling out for their prizes.

Alice had no idea what to do, she felt in her pocket and found a bag of sweets and handed them round as prizes. There was exactly one sweet each. They all cheered and took their sweets.

"But Alice must have a prize herself," said the mouse.

"What else do you have?" asked the Dodo.

Alice felt in her pocket, "Only a thimble," she said.

"Give it to me," said the Dodo.

All the animals crowded round her as the Dodo presented her with the thimble. As soon as he had done that they all began to wander off and soon Alice was left alone.

The Rabbit Sends
in a Little Bill

Alice began to cry again for she felt very lonely.
After a while she heard the pattering of footsteps
in the distance. She looked up eagerly hoping to see
the animals and birds returning, but it was the
White Rabbit trotting slowly back again. It seemed
to be looking for something, Alice heard it
muttering to itself, "The Duchess! The Duchess! Oh
my dear paws! Oh my fur and whiskers! She'll get me
executed. Where can I have dropped them, I wonder?"

Alice guessed right away that the Rabbit was
looking for his fan and his white gloves and she
started to help look for them, but they were nowhere
to be seen, everything seemed to have changed since
her swim in the pool, the great hall with the table
and the little door had completely disappeared.

Very soon the Rabbit noticed Alice as she was hunting about, and called out to her in an angry voice, "Mary Ann, what are you doing out here? Run home this minute and fetch me a pair of gloves and a fan! Quickly!"

Alice was so frightened that she ran off in the direction that the Rabbit was pointing in, without explaining the mistake that the Rabbit had made.

"He thought I was his house-maid," thought Alice as she ran. "How surprised he will be when he finds out who I really am. I had better take him his fan and gloves, that is if I can find them." She soon came upon a little house with a brass plate on the door which read "W. RABBIT". She went in without knocking and hurried upstairs in case she should meet the real Mary Ann.

"How strange it seems to be running an errand for a rabbit," said Alice to herself.

Alice had found herself in a tidy little room with a table by the window, and on it, as she had hoped there would be, a fan and two or three pairs of white gloves. She picked up the fan and a pair of the white gloves and was just about to leave the room when she saw a little bottle on the table. There was no label saying drink me, but Alice was sure that something interesting would happen so she uncorked the bottle and started to drink.

Before she had even drunk half of the bottle her head was pressing against the ceiling. She quickly put down the bottle hoping that she would not grow any more. She realised that at this size she would not be able to get out through the door. "I wish I had not drunk so much!" thought Alice.

It was too late to wish that! She went on growing and very soon had to kneel on the floor, in another minute there was not even room for her to do this, so she had to lay on the floor with one elbow against the door and the other arm was curled round her head. But she still continued to grow and as a last resort she had to put one arm out of the window and one foot up the chimney and hope that she did not grow any more.

"Now I can do no more," she said, unhappily.

Luckily for Alice she grew no larger, still it was very uncomfortable and as there seemed to be no way of ever getting out of the room again, she was very unhappy.

"It was much nicer at home," thought poor Alice. "I was not growing larger and smaller all the time there, and I wasn't being ordered around by mice and rabbits. I almost wish that I had not gone down that rabbit-hole – but it is strange that this sort of thing can happen. I wonder what can have happened to me. When I used to read fairy-tales, I used to hope this kind of thing would happen and now it has! It seems that I am in the middle of a fairy-tale myself. Perhaps when I grow up I will write a book about what has happened to me!"

After a few more minutes of thinking, Alice heard a voice outside, and she stopped to listen.

"Mary Ann! Mary Ann!" said a voice. "Fetch my gloves this instant!" Then came a pattering of feet on the stairs. Alice knew it was the Rabbit looking for her and she trembled till the house shook, quite forgetting that as she was about a thousand times as large as the Rabbit, there was no reason to be afraid.

The Rabbit came to the door and tried to open it but Alice's elbow was pressed hard against it and he could not get in. Alice heard it say to itself, "Then I'll go round and get in through the window."

"Oh no you won't," thought Alice, and she waited until she heard the Rabbit by the window and she made a sudden snatch in the air with her hand. She heard the Rabbit shriek and then heard its angry voice, "Pat! Pat! Where are you?"

"I'm here your honour, digging for apples," said a strange voice that Alice assumed belonged to Pat.

"Come here and help me," said the Rabbit. "Tell me what you think that is at the window."

"It's an arm, your honour," said Pat.

"How can it be an arm, look at the size of it! It fills the whole window!" snapped the Rabbit.

"I know," said Pat, "but it is an arm."

"Well it should not be there, please get rid of it," said the Rabbit.

20

There was a long silence after this, and Alice could only hear whispers, now and then, such as, "I don't like it, your honour!" and "Do as I tell you, you coward!" So Alice made another snatch in the air and this time there were two shrieks.

Alice waited for some time before she heard anything else, it was the sound of many little voices. Most of them were talking to someone called Bill. "Here Bill, catch hold of this rope, then you can swing down the chimney," said one of the voices.

"Oh," said Alice, "so Bill has got to come down the chimney has he? I do not think I would like to be Bill at the moment. This fireplace is very narrow but I think I can still kick a little!"

She moved her foot to make sure. She drew her foot as far down the chimney as possible and waited until she heard a little animal scrambling about in the chimney close to her foot.

"This must be Bill," she said to herself, and gave a sharp kick and waited to see what happened next.

The first thing she heard was a chorus of, "There goes Bill!" and then she heard all the animals outside talking together.

At last came a feeble, squeaking voice, that Alice thought must be Bill's. "Well," he said. "Something came up from under me and the next thing I knew I was flying through the air like a rocket."

"We must burn the house down," said the Rabbit.

"Oh no you won't," shouted Alice at once. There was an instant silence, and Alice thought to herself "I wonder what they will do next! If they had any sense they would take the roof off."

After a minute or two they began moving around again, and Alice heard the Rabbit say, "A barrowful will do to begin with."

"A barrowful of what?" thought Alice. But she did not have to wait long to find out for Alice felt a sharp sting on her face and then another followed by lots of little stings. She soon realised that they were throwing hundreds of pebbles at her. To her surprise the pebbles were turning into cakes as they hit the floor. Alice started to eat them, praying they would make her smaller.

The first thing she heard was a chorus of, "There goes Bill!"

To her delight she began to shrink. As soon as she was small enough to get through the door, she ran out of the house, and found a large crowd of little animals and birds waiting outside. The poor little Lizard, Bill, was laying on the grass in the middle. They all rushed at Alice, but she ran as fast as she could and found herself safe in a thick wood.

"The first thing I must do is grow back to my right size. Then I must find my way into that lovely garden," thought Alice.

Alice looked all around her. "Let me see," she said. "I think I must eat or drink something to make me grow, but the question is what?"

Alice looked all round her at the flowers and blades of grass, but she could not see anything that looked right to eat or drink. There was a large mushroom growing near her, about the same size as herself and when she had looked under it, on both sides of it and behind it, Alice thought that she might as well look on top of it.

She stretched herself on tiptoe and peeped over the edge, and her eyes immediately met those of a large blue caterpillar, that was sitting with its arms folded not taking any notice of her or of anything else.

24

Advice from a Caterpillar

The Caterpillar and Alice looked at each other for a long time in silence. At last the Caterpillar spoke.

"Who are you?" said the Caterpillar in a rather nasty voice.

Alice was a bit annoyed at the tone of the Caterpillar's voice. "I think you should tell me who you are first," she said.

"Why?" said the Caterpillar.

Alice could not think of a good reason and as the Caterpillar did not seem to be very friendly Alice turned and walked away.

"Come back!" shouted the Caterpillar. "I have something important to tell you."

Alice thought that as she had nothing better to do, she might as well wait and find out if what the Caterpillar had to say was worth hearing.

"What is it?" asked Alice.

"Do you like being the size you are?" it asked.

"No, not really," answered Alice. "I would like to grow a little bit. It's not much fun only being three inches high."

"What size do you want to be?" the Caterpillar asked.

"Oh I don't mind being any size as long as I don't keep changing," said Alice.

"You will get used to it in time," said the Caterpillar. It got down from the mushroom and began to walk away, merely remarking as it went, "One side will make you taller and the other side will make you shorter."

"What side of what? The other side of what?" thought Alice to herself.

"Of the mushroom," said the Caterpillar, as if he had heard her aloud.

Alice looked at the mushroom for a minute, trying to work out which were the two sides. As the mushroom was round it was very difficult to tell. Alice stretched her arms round the mushroom and broke a piece off with both hands.

"And now which is which?" she said to herself. She nibbled a piece of the right-hand piece and the next moment her chin hit her foot. She was very frightened by this and took a bite of the left-hand piece. Suddenly her head was free, but to Alice's horror her shoulders were nowhere to be seen. Her head was above the trees and she had an enormous neck. So next she tried eating a little of one and a little of the other until she was the right size again.

She wandered through the wood until she came across a tiny house about four feet high.

"Whoever lives there?" thought Alice. "If they see me at this size they will be scared out of their wits. I will make myself as small as they are." She began nibbling at the right-hand piece of mushroom until she was nine inches high.

Pig and Pepper

For a minute or two she stared at the house wondering what to do next when a fish dressed as a footman came running out of the wood and knocked loudly at the door. It was opened by a frog dressed as a footman.

The Fish-Footman produced a great letter, almost as large as himself and he handed it to the Frog-Footman, saying, "For the Duchess. An invitation from the Queen to play croquet."

The Frog-Footman took the letter and the Fish-Footman left. When Alice decided to go to the house the Frog-Footman was sitting outside staring stupidly into the sky.

Alice knocked on the door.

"There is no use in knocking," said the Frog-Footman. "They are making so much noise in there no one will hear you."

There certainly was a noise going on. A loud howling and sneezing, and every now and then a great crash, as if a dish or kettle had been broken into pieces.

At this moment the door of the house opened, and a large plate came skimming out. Alice took the chance to enter the house while the door was open and slipped in. The door led right into a large kitchen, which was full of smoke. The Duchess was sitting on a stool in the middle, holding a baby, the cook was leaning over the fire, stirring a cauldron which seemed to be full of soup.

The Duchess and the baby kept sneezing, the only two creatures in the kitchen that did not sneeze were the cook and a large cat, which was lying on the hearth, grinning from ear to ear.

Alice decided to speak. "Please can you tell me why your cat grins like that?" she asked.

"It's a Cheshire-Cat," said the Duchess, "that's why, Pig!"

Alice was quite offended until she saw that the last word was addressed to the baby and not her.

"There's too much pepper in that soup," said Alice.

The cook took the cauldron of soup off the fire, and started throwing everything she could lay her hands on at the Duchess and the baby. The Duchess took no notice even when they hit her, and the baby was howling so much already it was difficult to say whether it was hurt or not.

"Oh please be careful!" cried Alice, who was quite concerned as to the baby's safety.

"Here, you take it then," the Duchess said to Alice, giving her the baby. "I am going to play croquet with the Queen." The cook threw a frying pan at her as she hurriedly left the room.

Alice found holding the baby very difficult. It kept wriggling around and snorting very loudly. She decided to take the baby outside to let it have some fresh air.

The cook took the cauldron of soup off of the fire and started
throwing everything she could lay her hands on at the Duchess and
the baby.

As they got outside the baby started to grunt. Alice looked at it very carefully. The baby had now started to look very strange, its nose was beginning to look like a snout, and its eyes were becoming very small. Alice looked around her to find someone who could help her but when she turned back to the baby it had turned into a pig. Alice put it down and it trotted into the wood.

Just then Alice noticed the Cheshire-Cat sitting in a tree nearby. It saw Alice and grinned.

"Cheshire-Cat," said Alice, "please could you tell me which way I should go?"

"That depends on where you want to go," the Cheshire-Cat answered.

"I don't really care," said Alice.

"Well it doesn't matter then, does it?" the Cheshire-Cat said.

"As long as I get somewhere," said Alice quickly.

"If you go in that direction," said the Cat, waving his right paw around. "You will come across the Hatter, and in that direction," the Cat said, waving the other paw, "you will find the March Hare. You could go and visit either of those, they are both mad."

"But I don't want to be among mad people," said Alice.

"Oh, you can't help that," said the Cat, "we're all mad here. I'm mad. You're mad."

"How do you know I'm mad?" asked Alice.

"You wouldn't have come here, otherwise," he said. "Are you going to play croquet with the Queen?"

"I would like to," said Alice, "but I have not been invited yet."

"You will see me there," said the Cheshire-Cat, and vanished.

Alice decided that she would go and find the March Hare. She thought as it was May, perhaps it would not be quite so mad.

She had not walked very far when she came across the March Hare's house. It was a very large house, so she nibbled a piece of the left-hand bit of mushroom and and when she was large enough she walked towards it rather timidly.

A Mad Tea-Party

There was a table under a tree in front of the
house. The March Hare and the Hatter were there
having tea at it, a Dormouse was sitting between
them, fast asleep. The other two were using it as
a cushion, resting their elbows on it, and talking
over its head.

"It must be very uncomfortable for the Dormouse,"
thought Alice, "only it's asleep, so I suppose it
doesn't mind."

The table was very big, but all three of them
were squashed up in one corner. "No room! No room!"
they cried out when they saw Alice coming.

"There is plenty of room," said Alice, and she sat
down in a big arm-chair at the end of the table.

"Have some wine," said the March Hare, politely.

Alice looked around the table, but there was nothing but tea. "I don't see any wine," she said.

"There isn't any," said the March Hare.

"Then it was not very nice of you to offer it," said Alice angrily.

"It wasn't very nice of you to sit down without being invited," said the March Hare.

"I didn't know it was your table," said Alice. "It is set for a great many more than three."

"Your hair needs a cut," said the Hatter. He had been looking at Alice for some time and this was the first thing he said.

"You should not say things like that," said Alice. "It is rude."

The Hatter opened his eyes wide at this but all he said was, "Why is a raven like a writing-desk?"

"We shall have some fun, now," thought Alice. "I think I can guess that," she said.

"Do you mean you can tell us the answer?" asked the March Hare.

"Yes," said Alice.

"Then you should say what you mean," the March Hare said.

"I do," said Alice. "At least I mean what I say, it's the same thing, you know."

"No it's not," said the Hatter. "Otherwise 'I see what I eat' would be the same as 'I eat what I see'."

"You might just as well say 'I like what I get' and 'I get what I like'," said the March Hare.

"You might just as well say," added the Dormouse, who seemed to be talking in its sleep, "that 'I breathe when I sleep' is the same as 'I sleep when I breathe'."

"It is the same thing to you," said the Hatter, and here the conversation stopped, and everyone was silent for a minute.

The Hatter was the first to break the silence. "What day of the month is it?" he said, turning to Alice, he had taken his watch out of his pocket and was shaking it every now and again, holding it to his ear.

"The fourth," said Alice.

"Two days wrong," sighed the Hatter. "I told you butter would not do it any good!" he added, looking angrily at the March Hare.

"It was the best butter," the March Hare replied.

"Yes, but some crumbs must have got in it as well," the Hatter grumbled. "You should not have put it in with a bread-knife."

The March Hare took the watch and looked at it gloomily, then he dipped it in his tea, because he could think of nothing better to do.

Alice had been looking over his shoulder with some interest. "What a funny watch," she said. "It tells the day of the month and not the time."

"The Dormouse is asleep again," said the Hatter, and he poured a little tea on its nose. The Dormouse shook its head impatiently, but did not open its eyes.

"Have you guessed the riddle yet?" the Hatter asked Alice.

"No, I give up," Alice replied. "What is it?"

"I haven't the slightest idea," said the Hatter.

"Nor I," said the March Hare.

"I think you should do something better with the time than to waste it asking riddles that have no answer," said Alice, angrily.

"If you knew Time as well as I do," said the Hatter. "You wouldn't be talking about 'it', it's 'him'."

"I don't know what you mean," said Alice.

"Of course you don't," said the Hatter, "I bet you have never even spoken to Time."

"Perhaps not," Alice said. "But I know that when I learn music, I have to beat time."

"That accounts for it then," said the Hatter. "He won't like being beaten. If you are friendly towards him, he would do almost anything you liked with a clock. For instance, suppose it were only nine o'clock in the morning, just time to start school, you would only have to whisper to Time and the clock would go round so fast that it would be one o'clock and time for dinner."

"That would be good," thought Alice.

Here the Dormouse began singing in his sleep "Twinkle, twinkle, twinkle, twinkle."

"You could keep it at one o'clock for as long as you like," said the Hatter.

"Is that the way you do it," asked Alice.

The Hatter shook his head. "We quarrelled last March, just before he went mad you know," he said pointing to the March Hare. "It was at a great concert given by the Queen of Hearts, I had to sing 'Twinkle, Twinkle, Little Bat'."

Here the Dormouse began singing in his sleep "Twinkle, twinkle, twinkle, twinkle." It went on so long that they had to pinch it to make it stop.

"Well I had hardly finished the first verse," the Hatter said, when the Queen shouted, "He's murdering the time! Off with his head! Now he won't do a thing I ask. It's always six o'clock now."

"Is that the reason there are so many tea-things set out here?" asked Alice.

"Yes, it is always tea-time and we've no time to wash the things," said the Hatter.

"So you keep moving round?" asked Alice.

"As a matter of fact I need a clean cup now," said the Hatter. "Let's all move one place on."

He moved on as he spoke, the Dormouse followed him, the March Hare moved into the Dormouse's place, and Alice, although she did not really want to, took the place of the March Hare. The Hatter was the only one who got any advantage from the move, Alice was a good deal worse off because the March Hare had just spilt milk over his plate.

The Dormouse fell asleep immediately, and the Hatter and the March Hare started to whisper together so Alice could not hear. She sat there for a few minutes but deciding that she did not want to be ignored, she got up and left the table. As the Dormouse was asleep and the other two were talking, no one noticed her leave.

She noticed that a nearby tree had a door leading right into it. Alice went through the door and found herself in the long hall, close to the glass table. She picked up the key and walked to the door. She nibbled the mushroom until she was about a foot high then at last walked through the little doorway into the beautiful garden.

The Queen's Croquet-Ground

As Alice entered the garden, she saw something very strange. There were three gardeners painting a white rose-tree, so it was red. She went a bit closer to watch them. As she moved nearer to them, they saw her and stopped what they were doing.

"Please can you tell me why you are painting the roses?" asked Alice.

Five and Seven said nothing, but looked at Two. So Two said, "Well, this should have been a red rose-tree, but we put a white one in by mistake. If the Queen finds out we will have our heads cut off. So we must do our best to hide it before the Queen comes to-" At this moment Five, who had been anxiously looking across the garden called out, "The Queen! The Queen!" and the three gardeners threw themselves on their faces. There was a sound of many footsteps, Alice looked round eager to see the Queen.

*Last of all in this grand procession came THE KING AND
QUEEN OF HEARTS.*

First came ten soldiers carrying clubs: these were all shaped like the three gardeners, oblong and flat, with their hands and feet at the corners. Next came ten courtiers, these were decorated all over with diamonds. After these came the royal children, there were ten of them, these were decorated all over with hearts. Next came the guests, mostly Kings and Queens, Alice saw the White Rabbit among them, it was smiling in a nervous manner and walked past without noticing her. Then followed the Knave of Hearts, carrying the King's crown on a velvet cushion, and last of all in this grand procession came THE KING AND QUEEN OF HEARTS.

Alice was wondering whether she should be laying down on her face like the three gardeners, but she could not remember ever hearing about such a rule at a procession, "and besides," she thought, "what would be the point if everyone had to lie down on their faces, so they couldn't see?" So she stood and waited.

When the procession came opposite to Alice, they all stopped and looked at her, and the Queen said, "What is your name, child?"

"My name is Alice, your Majesty," said Alice very politely. "Why, they are only a pack of cards, so I have no reason to be afraid of them," she added to herself.

"And who are these?" she said, pointing to the three gardeners who were lying face down around the rose-tree.

"How should I know," said Alice. She was very surprised to hear herself sound so rude. "It's none of my business."

The Queen turned red with fury, and after staring at Alice for some time she began screaming, "Off with her head! Off with her head!"

"This is nonsense!" said Alice very loudly. "What have I done that is so bad that I need to have my head cut off?"

The Queen was so shocked at being spoken to in that way, that she turned angrily to the Knave and said, "Turn them over!"

40

The Knave did so very carefully, with one foot.

"Get up!" the Queen screeched, and the three gardeners instantly jumped up, and began bowing to the King, the Queen, the royal children and everyone else.

"Stop doing that!" screamed the Queen. "You're making me giddy," then turning to the rose-tree she went on, "and what have you been doing here?"

"Your Majesty," said Two. "We were trying . . ."

"I see," said the Queen, who had been examining the roses. "Off with their heads." The procession moved on, three guards stayed behind for the execution of the three gardeners who ran to Alice for protection.

"You won't have your heads cut off," said Alice, and she put them in a large flower-pot that was nearby. The guards searched around for a minute or two and then hurried off to join the others.

"Are their heads off?" shouted the Queen.

"Their heads are gone, your Majesty!" shouted the guards in reply.

"Good!" said the Queen. "Can you play croquet?"

The guards were silent and looked at Alice. Alice thought she had better answer even though she did not know if the Queen was talking to her so she shouted, "Yes!"

"Come on then," shouted the Queen. "Join the procession."

"It's a very fine day," said a timid voice by Alice's side. It was the White Rabbit.

"Yes," she said. "Where's the Duchess?"

"Hush! Hush!" said the Rabbit in a quiet voice. He looked over his shoulder as he spoke, then he went up on his tiptoes so his mouth was close to her ear and whispered, "She's under sentence of execution."

"What for?" asked Alice.

"Did you say 'What a pity!'?" the Rabbit asked.

"No I did not," said Alice. "I don't think it is a pity at all."

"She boxed the Queen's ears," the Rabbit said. Alice gave a scream of laughter. "Oh, hush!" the Rabbit whispered. "The Queen will hear you."

"Get to your places!" shouted the Queen in a voice of thunder. People ran in all directions and soon the game was underway.

Alice thought she had never seen such a curious croquet-ground in all her life, it was all ridges and furrows, the croquet balls were live hedgehogs, and the mallets live flamingoes. The guards had to bend over and stand on their hands and feet to make the arches.

Alice found it very difficult to hold the flamingo. Every time she sorted herself out and was about to hit the hedgehog, the flamingo would turn its neck and look at her with such a puzzled expression on its face that Alice could not help laughing. By the time she had actually got its head down, the hedgehog would have unrolled itself and crawled away. Alice soon came to the conclusion that it was a very difficult game to play.

The Queen was playing in a furious passion, and shouted "Off with his head!" or "Off with her head!" every minute or so.

Alice was beginning to get very worried about what would happen if the Queen said that to her, when she noticed something strange in the sky. It puzzled her at first but after looking at it more closely she made it out to be a grin, and she said to herself, "It's the Cheshire-Cat. Now I shall have someone to talk to."

"How are you getting on?" asked the Cat, when its mouth had fully appeared.

Alice waited until the eyes appeared. "It's no use talking to it until its ears have come otherwise it won't be able to hear me." In another minute the whole head appeared. Alice put down her flamingo, and began an account of the game, feeling very glad that there was someone to listen to her.

"They don't play very fairly," said Alice. "They all argue with each other, sometimes it is so loud that you can't hear yourself speak. There doesn't seem to be any rules and if there are, nobody takes any notice of them. It's all very confusing."

"How do you like the Queen?" said the Cat in a low voice.

42

"Not at all," said Alice, "she's so extremely–" Just then she noticed that the Queen was standing just beside her and went on, "–likely to win, it's hardly worth finishing the game."

The Queen smiled and moved on.

"Who are you talking to?" asked the King, looking at the Cheshire-Cat's head with great curiosity.

"It's a friend of mine – a Cheshire-Cat," said Alice.

"I don't like the look of it," said the King. "However it may kiss my hand if it likes."

"I'd rather not," the Cat remarked.

"How rude!" said the King. "And don't look at me like that." He stood behind Alice as he spoke.

"A cat may look at a king," said Alice. "I read that in a book somewhere."

"It must be removed," said the King very decidedly, and he called to the Queen who happened to be passing.

"My dear, I would like you to have this cat removed."

The Queen had only one way of settling all difficulties. "Off with his head!" she said without even turning round.

A large crowd had gathered round the Cheshire-Cat by now. An argument began to take place between the King, the Queen and the executioner.

The executioner said that you could not cut off a head unless there was a body. The King said that anything that had a head could be beheaded. The Queen said that if something was not done about it soon, everyone would be executed.

Alice could not think of a way to solve the argument, so she said, "It belongs to the Duchess, so you had better ask her."

"She's in prison," said the Queen. "Someone fetch her." The Cat began to fade away, and by the time the Duchess had arrived the Cat had completely disappeared.

The King and the executioner spent a long time running wildly up and down trying to find where it had gone, while the rest of the party went on with the game.

The Mock Turtle's Story and The Lobster-Quadrille

"I am glad to see you again, you dear old thing!" said the Duchess, tucking her arm into Alice's, and they walked off together.

Alice was glad she was in a better mood than when they had met before, she thought that perhaps it was only the pepper that had made her so bad-tempered when they had met in the kitchen.

"When I'm a Duchess," she said to herself, "I won't have any pepper in my kitchen at all. Soup tastes nice without it. Maybe it is pepper that makes all people bad-tempered," she went on, "and vinegar that makes them sour, and barley sugar that makes them sweet-tempered. I only wish people knew all this."

She had forgotten the Duchess by this time, and was a little startled when she heard her voice close to her ear.

"You're thinking about something, my dear," said the Duchess, "and that is making you forget to talk. I can't remember what the moral of that is, but I shall remember in a minute."

"Perhaps there isn't one," said Alice.

"Tut, tut!" said the Duchess. "Everything has a moral, if only you can find it." And she squeezed herself close to Alice as she spoke.

Alice did not like keeping so close to the Duchess, first, because the Duchess was very ugly and second, because the Duchess was exactly the right height to rest her sharp chin on Alice's shoulder. It was very uncomfortable, but Alice did not like to be rude, so she didn't say anything and let the Duchess stay where she was.

"The game's getting along better," said Alice, trying to make conversation.

"T'is so," said the Duchess. "And the moral of that is – 'Oh, 'tis love, 'tis love, that makes the world go round!' I bet you are wondering why I don't put my arm around your waist. The reason is, I'm a bit worried about the temper of your flamingo. Do you think I should try it?"

"He might bite," Alice replied, not wanting the Duchess to put her arm around her waist.

"Very true," said the Duchess, "flamingoes and mustard both bite. And the moral is – 'Birds of a feather flock together.'"

"But mustard isn't a bird," said Alice.

"Right as usual," said the Duchess. "What a clear way you have of putting things."

"It is a vegetable," said Alice, "it doesn't look like one, but it is."

Here, to Alice's great surprise the Duchess did not remark and the arm that was linked to hers began to tremble. Alice looked up, and there stood in front of them was the Queen, with her arms folded, frowning like a thunderstorm.

"A fine day, your Majesty," the Duchess said in a low, timid voice.

"I am giving you fair warning," shouted the Queen, stamping on the ground as she spoke, "either you or your head must be off. Take your choice."

The Duchess was gone in a moment.

"Let's get on with the game," the Queen said to Alice, and Alice was too frightened to say a word, but followed her back to the croquet-ground.

All the time they were playing the Queen never stopped quarrelling with the other players. She sentenced nearly every player to have his or her head cut off. Those who were sentenced were taken into custody by the guards, who had to leave off from being arches to do so. After about half an hour of this, there were no arches left and all the players apart from the King, the Queen and Alice, were in custody and under sentence of execution.

The Queen turned to Alice and said, "Have you seen the Mock Turtle yet?"

"No," said Alice. "I don't even know what a Mock Turtle is."

"Come on then," said the Queen, "and he will tell you his story."

As they walked off together, Alice heard the King say in a low voice, "You are all pardoned."

Alice and the Queen soon came across a Gryphon, laying fast asleep in the sun.

"Up, lazy thing!" said the Queen, "and take this young lady to see the Mock Turtle, and to hear his story. I must go back and see to some executions I have ordered."

Alice did not like the look of the Gryphon, but she thought she was probably safer staying with it than going back with such a savage Queen.

The Gryphon sat up and rubbed its eyes, then it watched the Queen until she was out of sight, then it chuckled.

"What fun!" said the Gryphon, half to itself and half to Alice.

"What is?" asked Alice.

"Why, the Queen, of course," said the Gryphon. "She never executes anyone you know. Come on."

They had not gone far before they saw the Mock Turtle in the distance, sitting sad and lonely on a rock. As they came nearer, Alice could hear him sighing as though his heart would break.

"What is the matter with him?" she asked the Gryphon.

"Nothing is the matter," answered the Gryphon. "Come on."

So they went up to the Mock Turtle who looked at them with large eyes full of tears. He said nothing.

"This young lady," said the Gryphon, "wants to know your story."

"Then I'll tell it to her," said the Mock Turtle. "Sit down both of you, and don't say a word until I have finished." He paused for a few minutes and then he began. "Once, I was a real Turtle. When I was little, I went to school in the sea. My master was an old Turtle, we used to call him Tortoise–"

"Why did you call him Tortoise, if he wasn't one?" Alice asked.

"We called him Tortoise because he taught us," said the Mock Turtle angrily. "Really you are very dull!"

"You ought to be ashamed of yourself, asking such a simple question," said the Gryphon, and then they both sat silent, staring at poor Alice. At last the Gryphon said to the Mock Turtle, "Carry on, old fellow," and the Mock Turtle continued.

"Yes, we went to school in the sea, we had the best education – in fact, we went to school every day."

"I go to school every day," said Alice. "So you needn't be so proud of that!"

"With extras?" asked the Mock Turtle.

"Yes," said Alice, "we learn French and music."

"And washing?" asked the Mock Turtle.

"Certainly not," said Alice.

"Then yours is not a really good school," said the Mock Turtle. "Now at ours, they had French, music and washing, extra."

47

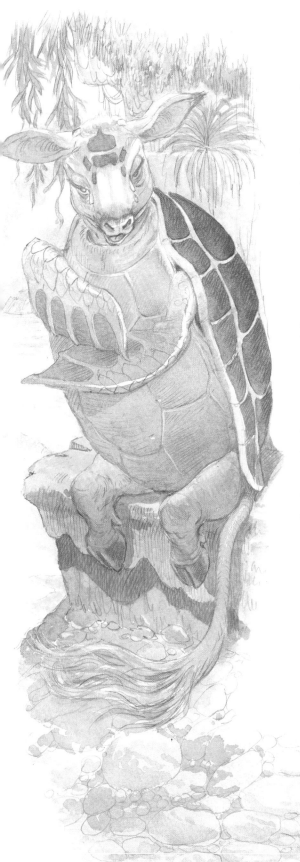

"You couldn't have needed it much," said Alice, "living at the bottom of the sea."

"I could not afford to learn it," said the Mock Turtle with a sigh. "I only took a regular course."

"What was that?" asked Alice.

"Reeling and writing, of course," the Mock Turtle replied, "and then some kinds of Arithmetic – Ambition, Distraction and Uglification."

"What is Uglification?" asked Alice. "I have never heard of it."

The Gryphon lifted up its paws in surprise. "Never heard of uglifying!" it exclaimed. "You know what to beautify is, I suppose?"

"Yes," said Alice. "It means to make things prettier."

"Well then," the Gryphon said, "if you don't know what to uglify is you are a simpleton."

Alice did not want to appear stupid, so she did not ask any more questions. Instead she turned to the Mock Turtle and said, "What else did you have to learn?"

"That's enough about lessons," the Gryphon interrupted in a very deciding voice. "Tell her something about the games now."

The Mock Turtle sighed deeply and looked at
Alice, he tried to speak, but sobs choked his
voice.

"It's the same as if he had a bone in his
throat," said the Gryphon and he started shaking
him and smacking him on the back. At last the Mock
Turtle found his voice, and, with tears running
down his face, he started.

"You may not have lived under the sea and may
not have been introduced to a lobster so you can
have no idea what a delightful thing a Lobster-
Quadrille is!"

"No indeed," said Alice. "Is it a kind of
dance?"

"Why yes," said the Gryphon. "You first form a
line along the seashore–"

"Two lines!" cried the Mock Turtle. "Seals,
turtles, salmon, and so on. Then when you have
cleared all the jelly-fish out of the way–"

"That takes quite a time," interrupted the Gryphon.

"–you advance twice-" the Mock Turtle continued.

"Each with a lobster as a partner!" cried the Gryphon.

"It must be a very pretty dance," said Alice.

"Would you like to see a little of it?" asked the Mock Turtle.

"Very much indeed," said Alice.

"Come on, let's try the figure," said the Mock Turtle to the Gryphon. "We can do it without lobsters. Who shall sing?"

"Oh you shall sing," said the Gryphon. "I have forgotten the words."

So they began dancing round and round Alice, every now and then treading on her toes when they passed too close.

They danced for quite a while and eventually stopped.

"Thank you, it's a very interesting dance to watch," said Alice. Secretly glad they they had finished.

"Come now," said the Gryphon to Alice. "Let's hear some of your adventures."

"I could tell you my adventures, beginning from this morning," said Alice. "But it's no use going back to yesterday because I was a different person then."

"Explain all that," said the Mock Turtle.

"No, no! The adventures first," said the Gryphon impatiently, "explanations take too long."

So Alice told them her adventures from when she first saw the White Rabbit. She was a little nervous at first because the two creatures were sitting so close to her, mouths and eyes open wide. Her listeners were perfectly quiet until a cry of, "The trial's beginning!" was heard in the distance.

"Come on!" cried the Gryphon, and, taking Alice by the hand, it hurried off.

"What trial is it?" Alice panted as she ran, but the Gryphon only answered, "Come on!" and ran even faster.

Who Stole the Tarts?

The King and Queen of Hearts were sitting on their throne when they arrived, with a great crowd gathered round them including the whole pack of cards. The Knave was standing before them, in chains, with a guard either side, and standing near the King was the White Rabbit.

In the very middle of the court was a table, with a large dish of tarts upon it, they looked very tasty and made Alice quite hungry whenever she looked at them.

Alice had never been in a court before, but she had read about them and was pleased to find out that she knew the name of everything there.

51

"That's the judge," said Alice, looking at the King. She could tell this from the wig he was wearing.

"And that's the jury-box, and those twelve creatures must be the jury."

"Herald, read the accusation!" said the King.

On this the White Rabbit blew three blasts on a trumpet, and then unrolled a parchment scroll, and read as follows:–

The Queen of Hearts, she made some tarts
All on a summers day:
The Knave of Hearts, he stole those tarts
And took them quite away!

"Consider your verdict," the King said to the jury.

"Not yet, not yet!" the Rabbit interrupted. "There is a great deal to come before that!"

"Call the first witness," said the King, and the White Rabbit blew three blasts on his trumpet and called out, "First witness!" The first witness was the Hatter.

"Take off your hat," the King said to the Hatter.

"It isn't mine," said the Hatter.

"Stolen!" exclaimed the King, turning to the jury who instantly wrote it down.

"I keep them to sell," the Hatter added as an explanation. "I've none of my own. I'm a hatter."

Here the Queen put on her spectacles and began staring hard at the Hatter, who turned pale and fidgeted.

"Give your evidence," said the King; "and don't be nervous, or I'll have you executed."

This did not encourage the witness at all, he kept moving from one foot to the other, looking uneasily at the Queen.

Just at this moment Alice felt a very curious sensation, she was growing larger again.

"I wish you wouldn't squeeze so," said the Dormouse, who was sitting next to her, "I can hardly breathe."

52

"I can't help it," said Alice, "I'm growing."

"You've no right to grow here," said the Dormouse.

All this time the Queen had not stopped staring at the Hatter, and, she said to one of the officers in the court, "Bring me the list of singers from the last concert!" on which the wretched Hatter trembled so, that he shook off both his shoes.

"Give your evidence," the King repeated angrily, "or I'll have you executed whether you are nervous or not."

"I'm a poor man," the Hatter began, in a trembling voice, "and I hadn't begun my tea – not above a week or so – and what with the bread and butter getting so thin – and the twinkling of the tea–"

"The twinkling of what?" said the King.

"It began with the tea," the Hatter replied.

"Of course twinkling begins with a T!" said the King sharply. "Do you think I'm stupid? Go on!"

"I'm a poor man," the Hatter went on, "and most things twinkled after that – only the March Hare said–"

"I didn't!" the March Hare interrupted in a great hurry.

"You did!" said the Hatter.

"I deny it!" said the March Hare.

"He denies it," said the King: "leave out that part."

"Well at any rate, the Dormouse said–" the Hatter went on, looking anxiously round to see if he would deny it too; but the Dormouse denied nothing, being fast asleep.

"After that," continued the Hatter, "I cut some more bread-and-butter–"

"But what did the Dormouse say?" one of the jury asked.

"That I can't remember," said the Hatter.

"If that's all you know about it, you may stand down," said the King.

"I can't go any lower," said the Hatter; "I'm on the floor now."

"I'm a poor man," the Hatter began, in a trembling voice.

"You may go," said the King, and the Hatter hurriedly left the court.

"Call the next witness!" said the King.

The next witness was the Duchess's cook. She carried the pepper-box in her hand, and Alice guessed who it was, even before she got into court, by the way the people near the door began sneezing all at once.

"Give your evidence," said the King.

"Shan't," said the cook.

The King looked at the White Rabbit, who said, "Your Majesty must cross-examine this witness."

"Well, if I must, I must," the King said, and after folding his arms and staring at the cook, he said in a low voice, "What are tarts made of?"

"Pepper, mostly," said the cook.

"Treacle," said a sleepy voice behind her.

"Collar that Dormouse!" the Queen shrieked. "Off with his head! Off with his whiskers!"

The whole court was in confusion by this time, trying to get the Dormouse out of court. By the time they had settled down, the cook had disappeared.

Alice watched the White Rabbit fumbling with his list, feeling very curious as to who the next witness would be, "for they haven't had much evidence yet," she said to herself. Imagine her surprise, when the White Rabbit read out, at the top of his shrill little voice, the name "Alice!"

"Here!" cried Alice, quite forgetting how large she had grown in the last few minutes. She jumped up in such a hurry that she knocked over the jury-box with the edge of her skirt, upsetting all the jurymen.

"Oh! I am sorry!" she cried, and she picked them all up again as quickly as she could.

"The trial cannot proceed," said the King, looking very hard at Alice, "until all the jurymen are back in their proper places."

Alice looked at the jury-box and saw that she had put the Lizard in upside-down. She soon put him the right way up.

"What do you know about this business?" the King said to Alice.

"Nothing," said Alice.

"Nothing at all?" said the King.

"Nothing at all," said Alice.

At this moment the King suddenly called out, "Silence!" he read from his book, "Rule Forty-two. All persons more than a mile high to leave the court."

Everybody looked at Alice.

"I'm not a mile high," said Alice.

"You are," said the King.

"Nearly two miles high," added the Queen.

"Well I shan't go at any rate," said Alice, "that's not a rule, you just invented it."

"It's the oldest rule in the book," said the King.

"Then it should be Number One," said Alice.

The King shut his book and turned to the jury. "Consider your verdict," he said in a quiet voice.

"There's more evidence," said the White Rabbit, jumping up in a great hurry, "this paper has just been picked up."

"What's in it?" said the Queen.

"A set of verses," answered the White Rabbit.

"Are they in the prisoner's handwriting?" asked one of the jury.

"No, they are not," said the White Rabbit.

"He must have copied somebody else's," said the King.

"That proves his guilt," said the Queen, "so off with his–"

"It does not prove anything of the sort!" said Alice. "Why, you don't even know what the verses are about."

"Read them," said the King.

The White Rabbit put on his spectacles. "Where shall I begin your Majesty?" he asked.

"Begin at the beginning," said the King.

There was silence in the court as the White Rabbit read out these verses:–

> They told me you had been to her,
>   And mentioned me to him:
> She gave me a good character,
>   But said I could not swim.
>
> He sent them word I had not gone,
>   (We know it to be true):
> If she should push the matter on,
>   What would become of you?
>
> I gave her one, they gave him two,
>   You gave us three or more;
> They all returned from him to you,
>   Though they were mine before.
>
> If I or she should chance to be
>   Involved in this affair,
> He trusts to you to set them free,
>   Exactly as we were.
>
> My notion was that you had been
>   (Before she had this fit)
> An obstacle that came between
>   Him, and ourselves, and it.
>
> Don't let him know she liked them best,
>   For this must ever be
> A secret, kept from all the rest,
>   Between yourself and me.

"Begin at the beginning," said the King.

"That's the most important piece of evidence we have heard yet," said the King, rubbing his hands; "so now let the jury–"

"If anyone of them can explain it," said Alice, (she had grown so large in the last two minutes, she was not afraid of interrupting him,) "I'll give him sixpence. I don't believe there's any meaning in it."

The jury all wrote down on their slates, "She doesn't believe there is any meaning in it," but none of them tried to explain the verse.

"If there is no meaning in it," said the King, "that saves a world of trouble, you know, as we need not try and find any. And yet I don't know," he went on, spreading out the verses on his knee, and looking at them with one eye; "I seem to see some meaning in them after all. '–*said I could not swim–*' you can't swim can you?" he added turning to the Knave.

The Knave shook his head. He was made of card so it was very unlikely that he would have been able to.

"All right so far," said the King. "'*I gave her one, they gave him two*' – why, that must be what he did with the tarts, you know–"

"But it goes on '*they all returned from him to you,*'" said Alice.

"Why, there they are!" said the King, pointing to the tarts on the table. "Nothing can be clearer than that. Let the jury consider their verdict," the King said, for about the twentieth time that day.

"No, no!" said the Queen. "Sentence first – verdict afterwards."

"Stuff and nonsense!" said Alice loudly. "The idea of having the sentence first!"

"Hold your tongue!" shouted the Queen.

"I won't!" said Alice.

"Off with her head!" the Queen shouted at the top of her voice. Nobody moved.

"Who cares for you?" said Alice (she had grown to her full size by this time). "You're nothing but a pack of cards!"

At this the whole pack rose up into the air, and came flying down upon her; she gave a little scream, half of fright and half of anger, and tried to beat them off, and found herself lying on the bank, with her head in the lap of her sister, who was gently brushing away some dead leaves that had fallen down onto her face.

"Wake up, Alice," said her sister. "Why, what a long sleep you have had!"

"Oh, I have had such a curious dream!" said Alice. And she told her sister as well as she could remember them, all these strange adventures of hers that you have just been reading about; and, when she had finished, her sister kissed her, and said, "It was a curious dream, dear, but now it's getting late. It must be nearly dinner-time."

So Alice got up and ran off, thinking while she ran, what a wonderful dream it had been.